PURE
AWESOME
PRESS

A brand of IVA PUBLISHING

Independently published by:
Bogdan Ivanov, dba IVA Publishing
Württembergische Str. 18
10707 Berlin
Germany

You can contact us at hello@ivapublishing.com

ISBN 9798440944886 (Paperback)

Cleaning Crew

Written by
Sophie Errante

Edited by
Davan ODonnell

Illustrated by
Ika N.

"The sun is out!" Crew said, "It's such a nice day!"
"Maybe we could go out and play!"

"But what should we do?
Oh, I've got it! We could visit the zoo!"

"We can see giraffes and a big cat,
The aquarium and the penguin habitat!
The zoo is my favorite place to go.
Please, please, don't say no!"

"Well, Crew, we would have fun at the zoo,"
Mom said, "But first, there are some things we must do."
"You must take a bath and make your bed,
Then brush every hair on your head."

"But why must we do that before having fun?
I don't want to take a bath. I want to skip and run!"

"Crew, we must take care of ourselves – everyone."

"Even the moon?" Crew asked. "Even the sun?"

"Yes, Crew, even the moon and the sun
Light up our world – they don't just have fun.
If you have a body, you must take care of it.
That includes having a strong mind and staying fit."

"How can I take care of my mind?"
Crew argued. "It's inside my head."
Mom replied, "You can start by making your bed."

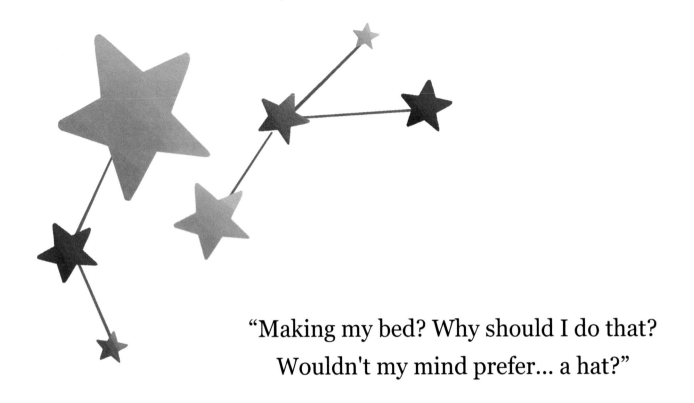

"Making my bed? Why should I do that?
Wouldn't my mind prefer... a hat?"

Mom replied, "When you go to bed tonight, you'll find
That pulling down fresh sheets relaxes your mind."

"So, before you start to have fun
Make sure your chores are properly done.
Brush your teeth and your hair, too.
Then, perhaps, we can go to the zoo."

"But why do I have to brush my hair?
Or wash my hands or find clean underwear?"

Mom replied, "All that is called hygiene.
It keeps us healthy and keeps us clean."

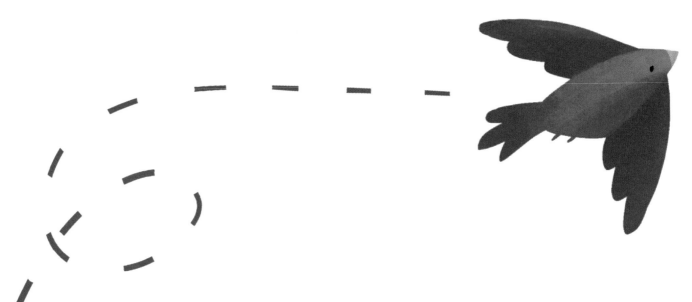

"What else must I do? Jumping and running?"
Crew asked excitedly. "Going to the pool and water-gunning?"

"No, not like that," Mom said. "More like flossing and brushing.
And being thorough without rushing.
And washing your face without scratching,
And making sure your socks are matching."

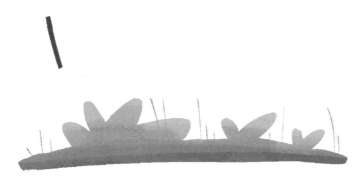

"Is hygiene fun things that I like?"
Crew asked. "Like riding a bike?"
"Not all thing about hygiene are fun,"
Mom replied. "But they simply must get done."

"I know, Crew! You can make it a game!
That way, chores and fun are the same.
Brush your teeth while making a funny face,
Or clean your room like you're in a race."

"I bet the animals at the zoo don't do that stuff,"
Crew stomped. "This is unfair, I've had enough!"
"The animals at the zoo practice hygiene, too.
It just might look different from what we do."

"The monkeys keep each other's hair bug-free,
While the birds groom to keep their feathers pretty.
The zookeepers feed the animals greens
And give them all vaccines."

"The penguins wash themselves with splashes,
and the zookeepers use soap to prevent rashes.
The zebras swipe their tails to keep flies away,
The elephants stay healthy by eating hay."

"So, all these animals have fun and play,
But they also keep clean every day.
Time for work and time for fun is key
If you want to be happy and carefree."

We can learn from anyone, even animals at the zoo.

We can even learn from Crew.

No matter how many things you have to do,

Chores and hygiene lead to a better you!

The End

THANK YOU!

for reading Cleaning Crew.
Please consider leaving us a
review on Amazon. Your
opinion is important to us!

Made in the USA
Las Vegas, NV
05 November 2024